The Sweet Outdoors

First Hardcover Edition, June 2023
First Paperback Edition, June 2023
10 9 8 7 6 5 4 3 2 1
FAC-004510-23103
Printed in the United States of America

This book is set in Aptifer/Linotype
Designed by Marci Senders

Library of Congress Cataloging-in-Publication
Control Number 2023930393

Hardcover ISBN 978-1-368-08147-4
Paperback ISBN 978-1-368-08145-0
Reinforced binding

Visit www.DisneyBooks.com

The Sweet Outdoors

SHARI SIMPSON

Illustrated by
SAOIRSE LOU

Disney • Hyperion

Los Angeles   New York

Chapter 1

"Sweet mother of monkey milk!" shouted Vanellope as she drove her animated truck through a gate that said YOU ARE NOW LEAVING BOLIVIARODRIGO.

"Woo-hoo!" Snowanna crowed, turning her steering wheel with relish. "I think we just entered ChilePepper!"

"Next up, EcuadoorBell!" Rancis yodeled from his peanut butter–colored SUV.

Ever since Vanellope Von Schweetz, Snowanna Rainbeau, Rancis Fluggerbutter, Minty Zaki, and Taffyta Muttonfudge accidentally got sucked out of their arcade game *Sugar Rush* in Game Central Station in Litwak's Family Fun Center and into the game tablet of ten-year-old Molly McGinty, they'd been having so many adventures!

Of course, being Racers and all, one of their

favorite things to do was drive in Molly's tablet game, *Race Around the Earth*, because it had the funniest pretend names of countries and towns (like France-y Pants, Turkey Leg, and the United States of Anime) and bodies of water (like the Red C and the Amazon Prime River).

Minty, who was driving a mint-green sports car, opened her mouth to yell something, too, but—

"Don't you dare!" Taffyta hissed at her from a pale pink convertible.

Ever since they'd raced through the city of Rhyme in the country of Ickily, Minty had been copying the Rhymians' silly rhyming words and phrases. And it was driving the other Racers *cuckoo*. Like, when Minty wanted to say "That's fun!" she'd say "Rat's bun!" instead. Or if she wanted to shout "Yay!" instead she'd shout "Neigh!"—leading them to think that a horse had somehow galloped into their game. Or, even now, she answered Taffyta with—

"Mutt pie bike sit!" Minty chortled.

"MINTY!" the Racers roared.

"Okay, okay." Minty giggled. "I was just trying to say 'But I like it.'"

"Yeah, but it's driving *us* wackadoodle," grumbled Taffyta.

Suddenly, there was a ginormous head looming above them, but the Racers weren't scared because the massive noggin belonged to their favorite live girl, Molly McGinty.

"What's driving you wackadoodle?" Molly asked, grinning.

"Bellow, Folly!" Minty could barely get this out, she was giggling so hard. Molly looked pretty confused as Minty rolled around in her driver's seat, laughing.

The Racers screeched to a halt so they could have an actual conversation.

Vanellope sighed. "That. *That.* Minty is trying to say 'Hello, Molly!'"

Now Molly laughed. "Oh, I get it! She's rhyming. It's kind of cute!"

Taffyta pulled her sweet strawberry lollipop out of her mouth and made the sourest of faces. "Please. Do not humor her."

Molly repositioned the tablet so she could look right at the Racers, and that's when they noticed how excited their friend looked. Molly's eyes were super shiny, and her smile was even wider than usual.

"Good golly, Miss Molly, you look happy," said Snowanna. "Like you just ate your way through King Candy's Castle."

"Even better than that, Snowanna!" Molly said. "'Cause, you know, too much sugar isn't good for you."

Taffyta stopped in mid-lolly-lick. "Huh?"

Molly didn't answer, because it wasn't easy to explain a healthy diet to characters that lived on ice cream and M&M's. "Anyway . . . the big news is: My Outdoor Scouts troop is going camping!"

"Awesome!" said Snowanna.

"Cool!" said Rancis.

"Nifty!" said Taffyta.

"Nice!" said Vanellope.

"Feet!" said Minty. The other Racers gave her a dirty look. "Fine, fine. Sweet!"

The Racers turned back to Molly and continued to smile for a long, awkward pause. Finally, Molly said:

"You don't know what camping is, do you?"

"Nope!" said Snowanna.

"Sure don't!" said Rancis.

"Not a clue!" said Taffyta.

"Wait, wait, wait," said Vanellope. "Me, Pyro, and Butcher Boy spent a night in a burned-out building in *Slaughter Race* once. We cooked wieners over the one lightbulb that was still working and sang songs about crushing our enemies. That's like camping, right?"

"Uh . . ." Molly hesitated. "Not quite. I mean, I've actually never camped myself, but Rio told me all about it."

Rio Rodriguez was Molly's best friend, and the Racers had become very fond of him. Of course, when they'd *first* met Rio, he and Molly were competing in the big Sweet River Go-Kart Race and were kinda mad at each other. So, naturally, it took the Racers a while to trust him, especially when they thought Rio had stolen the plans for Molly's go-kart design and Taffyta kept shrieking that he was a TFF (Totally Fake Friend). But now, all was forgiven and they genuinely liked Rio, even though they thought it was a little, um, *unusual* that he celebrated Halloween all year long; like, even on Earth Day, when he hung eco-friendly plastic spiders in his living room window.

"So, you sleep in a tent, and hike in the woods, and cook your food outside." Molly's voice was rising as she got more pumped up by the moment. "And it's still too early to swim in the lake, but you get to *sit* by the lake and *look* at the lake! Isn't that awesome?"

"Super awesome!" said Rancis.

"In *Sugar Rush*, we have Diet Cola Mountain!" said Minty, forgetting to rhyme in her excitement. "It's a volcano full of boiling hot cola so you can't swim in it either because you'd melt! Is your lake like that?"

Molly opened her mouth to answer Minty, then decided to just keep going. "Rio did tell me one thing that's kind of *not* awesome, though. We're going on the camping trip with the Outdoor Scouts from Shady Brook, which is the town next to Sweet River. And he says they're"—Molly lowered her voice and made it super dramatic—"the *enemy.*"

"Ooooooh," said the *Sugar Rush* Racers, making their voices low and super dramatic, too.

Now Molly opened her eyes wide and leaned in so close to the tablet that her mouth disappeared, but the Racers could still hear her talking in her low, super-dramatic voice. "On last year's camping trip, the Shady Brook Scouts played all sorts of pranks on our troop."

The Racers shivered and nodded knowingly. A prank was something they understood, having played them in *Sugar Rush* many times.

"Did they fill your car's gas tank with melted chocolate?" whispered Snowanna.

Molly had to think about this for a moment. "No, but they put a rubber snake on Timmy and Tommy Lang's fishing pole and the twins almost fell into the lake, and they put rocks in the supplies backpack and Rio didn't know why it was so heavy when he carried it on the hike, and when my troop was asleep in their tents, the Shady Brookers snuck in and painted their faces like clowns—"

"Bulging bags of Bozo bagels, that's terrible!" exclaimed Vanellope.

Rancis trembled with rage, his peanut butter cup jiggling on his head. "Something needs to be done about these monsters!"

"Good thing you got us, Molly," said Snowanna. "We know more prank paybacks than any other game characters at Litwak's, and that includes the dudes from *Stop 'Em & Top 'Em!*"

Taffyta started to tug at her fingers. "Yes! Somebody hold my gloves!"

"Um, guys?" Molly bit her lip, looking a bit nervous. "I'm super-duper sorry about this, but our troop leaders want us to enjoy the great outdoors and all that, so . . . no electronic devices are allowed on the camping trip."

Minty's eyes went wide. "Pee ant dumb?!"

The other Racers were too shocked to scold Minty, and, besides, Molly was a decent rhymer and had already figured it out. "That's right, Minty. You can't come."

What?!

Chapter 2

"K iss winks!"

Molly groaned. The McGintys and Rio were shopping at Biff's Camping and Outdoor Furniture Emporium, and no matter how low Molly turned the volume down on her tablet, she and Rio could still hear every single rhyme of "This stinks!" that Minty came up with.

"You're right, Minty, it does stink that you guys can't come on the camping trip," whispered Rio patiently. He was hiding out in a two-person pop-up tent that was on display so he could try to keep the Racers calm. "Um, can someone give Taffyta a tissue?" he asked.

Vanellope barely looked at the mascara streaming down Taffyta's face; she was too busy pacing back and forth across the tablet's home screen. "Catastrophic campfires on a crunchy

cracker! There's gotta be *something* we can do!" Vanellope grumbled. "We can't let Molly go by herself into the woods with the supershady Shady Brookers!"

"Waaahhhh!" wailed Taffyta.

Molly looked around at the other shoppers anxiously. "Guys, for real, I'm gonna have to put you on 'mute' if you don't chill out—" She stopped abruptly as her dad, Pete, trotted over with a huge smile on his face.

"Isn't this place the greatest?" said Pete happily. "I wish your mom liked camping, but ... oh, well!"

Molly and Pete looked over at Penny, who was having her own fun examining the fancy lawn furniture display. Molly's mom had always declared herself a "nice hotel and heated swimming pool kind of girl," so Pete accepted that sleeping on the ground in the woods was never going to be Penny's style.

"Time plaid!" came a teeny voice from the pop-up tent, followed by Snowanna's voice. "We know you're sad, Minty! Just quit rhyming about it!"

Molly and Rio froze, but Pete had spied a yellow camping hammock that looked like a giant banana and was already on the move to go lie down in it. Molly collapsed next to Rio inside the pop-up tent with a frustrated sigh.

"Are you sighing, Molly?" called out Vanellope. "Sweet mother of monkey milk, you're making her sigh with all that rhyming, Minty! Knock it off!"

"I'm sorry, Molly," Minty said. "I'll stop rhyming if it's crushing your soul."

Molly had to laugh a little. "Uh, no, it's not crushing my soul, Minty."

"Bunderful!" cried Minty.

Taffyta made a face. "Now *I'm* sighing."

Rio was shifting the tablet from one hand to the other and biting his lip. "Um . . . speaking about crushing souls, Moll . . . I have to tell you another not-awesome thing. . . ."

"Oh, no," Molly groaned. "Now what?"

"Well, since Shady Brook has two girls in their troop—"

Molly bolted up so quickly, she banged her head on the inside roof of the tent. "What?! The Shady Brook troop has girls in it?!"

"Yeah, Keiko and Felicia, so don't be mad—"

"Why would I be mad about that?!" Molly exclaimed, rubbing her ouchy scalp. "They may be the enemy, but still, you know I'm all about girl power!"

"Us, too!" chorused the Racers, including Rancis, who was very pro-girl.

Rio gritted his teeth. "Let me finish my sentence, okay?!"

"Oh. Sorry, Rio. You're right," said Molly, sheepishly settling back down next to him. Sometimes, even best friends can misunderstand each other, especially when they have a group of game characters chiming in every two seconds.

"Anyway, since you three are the only girls . . . you're going to have to share a tent with them."

Molly's mouth dropped open. She was speechless. But the Racers weren't.

"Whaaaa?!" gasped Rancis, too upset to even add the *t*.

"Our girl has to bunk with the *enemy*?!" Snowanna thundered.

Taffyta burst into fresh tears. And there was still no tissue.

"Parable!" wailed Minty, which was either "Terrible!" or "Unbearable!" or maybe both.

But Vanellope had a different reaction. She chuckled. "Guys, you're thinking about it all wrong. This could be a *good* thing."

Molly finally found her voice. "How?" she squeaked out.

"Yeah, how?" said Rio, eager to not be the deliverer of bad news.

Vanellope did that Vanellope thing of putting her tiny hands on her hips and waggling her head back and forth. "When I was hanging out with the Disney Princesses—"

Taffyta stopped crying long enough to roll her eyes. "I knew she was going to pull the Princesses into this somehow."

"—I did the regal gals a big fat favor," Vanellope continued, as if she hadn't heard Taffyta. "I eavesdropped on Lumiere, Mushu, and GusGus and found out they were going to TP the castle—"

"No offense, V.," said Snowanna. "But why does a bunch of Disney sidekicks doing dumb stuff with toilet paper apply to Molly's situation?"

"*Because*, Snow, my little doubter," Vanellope said, strutting a bit. "If Molly is sharing a tent, she can listen in on the private conversations of Kittycat and Felipe—"

"Um, Keiko and Felicia—" murmured Rio.

"Yeah, whatever, and find out what pranks the shady Shady Brookers are planning!" Vanellope grinned triumphantly. "Amirite?!"

Taffyta wiped off some mascara and gave Vanellope a grudging nod. "That's so sneaky, I'm sad I didn't think of it myself."

Snowanna and Rancis double-fist-bumped Vanellope. "Brilliant."

"Spice!" said Minty, and no one forced her to say "Nice!" instead.

"Thank you, thank you very much," said

Vanellope, taking a small bow. "And not to be too big for my britches or anything, but my genius ideas are just another reason Molly needs us on this camping trip!"

"Oh, for the love of Pete . . ." sighed Molly.

Right on cue, Pete stuck his head into the tent. "My favorite expression!" He was smiling and chewing what looked like a piece of old leather. "Everything okay, honey?"

"Yeah, totally, Dad," Molly said, managing a smile back.

"Oh, good," Pete said. "Jerky?"

"Huh?" said Rio.

Pete held out another piece of the leathery brown stuff. "They're giving out free samples of vegan jerky. I swear, it tastes just like meat!"

"And looks like an old shoe," came a voice from the general direction of Molly's tablet. Molly quickly thrust it behind her back. "SO!" she said brightly. "Having fun, Dad?"

"Too *much* fun, actually," said Pete. "Do you

realize we've been here for an hour already and I haven't bought a single item on our list?"

Rio and Molly looked at each other, surprised. It hadn't felt like they'd been at the camping store for an hour, but if they added up all of Minty's rhymes, the numerous instances of Taffyta either bursting into tears or bossing everyone around, and how many times Vanellope said "Sweet mother of monkey milk!" well ... maybe Pete was right.

"We need to get a little teamwork going," Pete said, swallowing down the last of his free jerky. "Teamwork makes the dream work!"

Molly and Rio looked at each other again, clueless. What did *that* mean?

"When you have a group that needs to accomplish a goal, it's a good idea to use the strengths of each person," said Pete, waving to Penny, who reluctantly pulled herself away from the crushed velvet patio chairs and came over to listen. "Since your mom is an architect, *she* can find the tent with the best construction.

And since Rio goes out to trick or treat on every major holiday—"

"And some of the minor ones, too!" said Rio happily.

"—And since he always uses a flashlight, he can choose the best one for Molly."

Molly's eyes lit up. "Can you find me a waterproof one, Rio?"

"Are you planning on swimming with it, Moll?" said Rio with a little huff. "Otherwise, it's best to just go with a basic model."

Molly resisted making a face at Rio as Penny said, "Pete, you should shop for Molly's sleeping bag, because you love to nap."

Pete grinned. "I do love a good power nap! And a catnap. And a three-hour nap after I mow the lawn. And . . . anyway, I'm getting off track here, what should Molly shop for?"

They all turned and looked at Molly. "Um . . ." she said, her forehead wrinkling. "I love cars, obvi."

"Not much need for a car on a camping trip," mused Pete.

Molly knew this would get a cry of outrage from the Racers, so she tucked the tablet up under her hoodie in the back.

"Molly likes to eat," said Rio. "She could shop for a mess kit."

"A mess kit?" questioned Molly, her forehead wrinkling a little bit more. "That sounds kind of gross."

Rio laughed. "It just means a portable plate and utensils."

"Oh. I guess I could do that."

Pete clapped his hands together. "Great! Let's meet back here in twenty minutes with our stuff. Remember, teamwork makes the dream work!"

Molly still didn't really know what that expression meant. And as she walked away with the Racers yelling from her backpack that cars are *perfect* for camping trips because you can roast a marshmallow over the engine, she still didn't feel like she was contributing much to the team. Or the dream.

ollllleeeee . . ." came a long whine from the tablet on her desk. "Pleeeeease . . ."

Molly grunted with effort (she was trying to zip her very full backpack closed) and frustration (she couldn't take the Racers' begging to go on the camping trip anymore). "Guys, you *know* I don't want to leave you here! But what can I do? It's the rules!"

"Rules are meant to be broken," said Taffyta.

Vanellope frowned. "Um, not a good life lesson for a human kid, Taff."

Snowanna stopped right in the middle of patting her snow-cone hair into place. "Wait. What if we could find a way to go on the trip *without* breaking any rules?"

"How would that work?" said Rancis.

Molly stopped trying to zip her backpack and

leaned over the tablet. "Yeah, I'm dying to hear this."

"Well, your backpack is open, right?" said Snowanna with a mischievous little grin. "It's not your fault that you have a lot of stuff in it and it's hard to zip."

Vanellope started nodding, "Yeah, yeah, yeah, I see where you're going with this!"

"Where?" said Taffyta in a bored voice.

"Yeah, where? 'Cause I don't get it," said Minty

in a somewhat petulant voice. The Racers had forbidden her to rhyme for five whole minutes and she was being a little pouty about it, to be honest.

But Rancis started getting worked up, his peanut butter cup hat trembling with excitement. "I get it! Because it wouldn't be *your* fault if we happened to bump the tablet into that unzipped knapsack, right?"

"Funwhipped flapjack?" whispered Minty, knowing she wasn't supposed to, but rhyming "funwhipped" with "unzipped" was just too tempting. Taffyta gave her a dirty look and Minty stuck her tongue out, just a tiny little bit.

Meanwhile, Molly had her hands over her ears. "La la la, I didn't hear that, Rancis!"

Vanellope pumped her tiny fist. "Good job, Molly! If you *hear* us, you'll be breaking the rules. But if you *don't* hear us, you're innocent!"

"Ohhhh," said Minty. "Ignorant."

The Racers were about to scold Minty, but

realized that it was actually a pretty good rhyme, because "ignorant" meant "not knowing." If Molly didn't "know" that the tablet was in her backpack, she wouldn't really be breaking the rules!

Now it was just a matter of getting the tablet into the backpack. Molly did her part—she went to go make her bed, leaving the backpack open. And the Racers decided that *their* part was a no-brainer: If they all ran toward the side of the tablet and bumped it at the exact same time, it would teeter and fall off the desk. Easy, right?

Not so much. Vanellope wanted to do a countdown so they'd all start running at the same time; Snowanna said they should just "freestyle"; Rancis and Taffyta started arguing when Rancis said he could just push the tablet over with his superstrong muscles and Taffyta rolled her eyes; and Minty kept asking when her five minutes were up, because she had some great rhymes for "Go!" ("Flow!" "Dough!" "Banjo!")

Finally, after Rancis hit his funny bone on the side of the tablet (which did *not* make him laugh but made Taffyta guffaw) and Snowanna freestyled her way right into the Volume button (making Minty's shouts of "Snow! Faux!" horribly loud), Vanellope put her tiny fingers in her tiny mouth and WHISTLED, long and shrilly. The Racers stopped and looked at her in surprise.

"Yeah, Butcher Boy taught me how to whistle to stop Pyro and Shank from arguing," Vanellope said. Then she bent over and put her hands on her knees, taking a deep breath. "Wooh! That takes a lot of oxygen."

"Are you going to pass out?" asked Taffyta, looking more delighted than she probably should have.

"No, Taff, I have excellent lung capacity," Vanellope said, straightening up. "When I was singing my 'heart song' after I met the Disney Princesses—"

Now Taffyta put *her* hands over her ears. "La la la, I didn't hear 'Princesses'!"

"Guys," said Snowanna sternly, "this is not the time to argue about royalty!"

"Yeah!" piped up Minty. "Molly needs us to think outside the game tablet!"

Lucky for all of them, Molly was dragging her sleeping bag across the floor at that very minute; she bumped her desk and the tablet fell into the open backpack! And it really was an accident, so no rules were broken! Of course, she had to pretend not to notice the Racers yelling "Whooooaaah!!!" as they flew downward and not listen when they yelled "Wheeeeee!" as she slung the backpack over her shoulder. And the Racers had to pretend Molly was talking to herself when she said, "Just a random thought, I sure would never want to get anyone else in trouble, especially someone with spiky hair who loves ghosts and goblins!" They got the message: Rio couldn't know that the Racers were coming on the camping trip because that would make him part of the rule-breaking.

After hugging Pete and Penny goodbye, Molly

ran down the sidewalk and hopped on the bus to a big group of boys shouting "Molly!" and "Hey, winner-winner-chicken-dinner!" (because she'd just won the Sweet River Go-Kart Race, obvi). She settled in next to Rio, who was wearing a T-shirt that said OCTOBER 31ST IS FOR AMATEURS. I CELEBRATE HALLOWEEN ALL YEAR LONG! But Molly didn't even get a chance to comment on the new shirt because Rio was in the middle of a heated conversation with Timmy and Tommy Lang, the twins who did absolutely everything at absolutely the same time, including talking, sighing, and scratching their blond mohawk haircuts.

"Hiking!" shouted Timmy and Tommy (together, of course).

Rio shook his head. "Scavenger Hunt!"

"Hot dogs roasted over an open fire!" shouted Timmy and Tommy. Molly was impressed, as usual, that the Lang twins could say even long sentences in perfect harmony.

"Sca—ven—ger—Hunt!" Rio yelled, drawing each syllable out.

"Hey, hey, what's the argument about?" asked Molly.

Rio shrugged. "We have this fight every year. Which part of camping is the best? But it shouldn't even be a question—the Scavenger Hunt rules."

"What's a Scavenger Hunt?" Molly asked innocently.

Suddenly, all noise on the bus stopped and every single Outdoor Scout turned to Molly with their mouths open. It was weird, sure, but Molly was a little distracted by just how many rubber bands were holding Timmy and Tommy Lang's braces in place in their wide-open mouths, so she didn't get upset.

"Molly, you've never been on a Scavenger Hunt before?" Timmy and Tommy asked in a hushed tone.

And then everyone started talking at once. From the bits and pieces that she could pick out, Molly guessed that Scavenger Hunt teams each got a list of items to collect out in the forest, simple stuff like a pine cone, a feather, something

round, a yellow flower, something that can make noise, stuff like that, and the first team to find all the items won. It was kind of confusing all coming in little sound bites, but it sounded pretty fun. And what made it even better was that Molly's troop was pretty pumped about winning, since the supershady Shady Brookers had won last year and this year was all about payback.

Then, suddenly—

"We're here!"

And every single Outdoor Scout ran to the side of the bus to see the shining lake, the dense trees, and their troop leader, Mr. Harrod, in funny hiking shorts that showed his knobby knees. A huge cheer rose up, so loud that no one even seemed to notice that some of the happiest and most excited yells came from inside Molly's backpack.

Chapter

4

At the camping site, Molly couldn't stop staring at the dense green trees and the clear
blue sky. Of course, she could see trees and sky
in her own backyard in Sweet River, but this was
different; there was so *much* sky and so *many*
trees.

The Racers, however, were rather unim-
pressed. Mostly because all *they* could see was
the inside of Molly's backpack.

"Mossglowboatik!" moaned Minty.

"Minty," said Snowanna, shaking her purple
head. "I've gotten to be a halfway decent rhymer,
but you stumped me on this one."

"She's claustrophobic," said Rancis glumly.

Taffyta pulled the lolly out of her mouth and
said in an annoyed voice, "Yeah. Still no clue."

Rancis took off his little brown jacket and

wiped his forehead dramatically. "'Claus-trophobic' means she feels like she can barely breathe and she's totally stuck in this backpack for, like, forever and ever and will never escape. Never, ever."

"Clever, Trevor!" wailed Minty.

They heard the *zzzzz* of the backpack zipper and light poured in, followed by Molly's face, which didn't look happy. "Guys, seriously!" she whispered. "You have to be quiet or I'm gonna get in big trouble—"

Suddenly, another voice, unfamiliar and high-pitched, said, "Whatcha doin'?"

Molly yanked her head out of the backpack and quickly turned to see two girls looking at her curiously. The taller girl, with stick-straight black hair and little round glasses, folded her arms. "Were you *talking* to your backpack?"

"Oh . . . uh . . . well . . ." fumbled Molly.

She was saved from having to answer by the shorter girl sneezing the most enormous, ground-shaking sneeze ever. Molly jumped.

"Felicia, can you warn us when you're gonna do that?!" exclaimed the taller girl. "You scared the snot outta me!"

"Sorry, Keiko!" Felicia the Sneezer said. "Allergies."

Molly casually dropped her backpack behind her and held out her hand. "I'm Molly."

Keiko looked at Molly's fingers with suspicion. "I don't want to shake that until I know if you can recognize a poison ivy plant. Two leaves or three?"

"Huh?" said Molly.

Felicia pulled a tissue out of her pocket and jammed it in one of her nostrils. "Keiko knows lots about camping. She knows how to climb trees, and put up a tent, and make a fire without matches. And she knows *everything* about poisonous plants, like if you touched poison ivy, you could spread it. Do you know if you touched poison ivy?"

Molly shook her head. "I haven't touched anything. I just got here."

"Well, okay," said Keiko. But instead of shaking Molly's hand, she kept her arms folded. "Still . . . I can't shake your hand because my troop says your troop is the enemy."

Molly scowled. "Oh, yeah? Well, *my* troop says *your* troop is the enemy."

Keiko matched her scowl. "So, that's how it's going to be, huh?"

Molly's scowl deepened. "That's how it's going to be!"

"Cat's wow splits growing booby!" came a tiny cry from the direction of the backpack behind Molly's feet, followed by a "Minty, sssshhhhhh!"

Keiko and Felicia looked confused. But before Molly could try to pretend that she was a ventriloquist and could "throw" her voice, she was saved by the appearance of Mr. Harrod, who now had a streak of white sunblock covering his nose.

"Girls, I see you've met already!" said Mr. Harrod happily. "How about that, Mrs. Apple?"

Mrs. Apple strode over, and Molly couldn't help thinking that Mrs. Apple's name fit her well, as the other troop leader was quite round and her face quite red. She was carrying an enormous (and enormously ugly) handbag and toted a little pug dog under her arm, who was almost as round as she was.

"Wonderful!" boomed Mrs. Apple. She looked down at the pug. "Isn't that wonderful, Mortimer?"

Mortimer looked back at her and snorted.

"I agree!" said Mrs. Apple, and she looked at Molly, Felicia, and Keiko. "Mortimer thinks you're going to be the best of friends before our trip is over!"

Molly doubted that, since Keiko was currently giving her a quite nasty side-eye and, below the tissue sticking out of her nose, Felicia's mouth was set in a straight, thin line. But somehow Molly knew that questioning Mortimer was probably not going to fly with Mrs. Apple.

"We're going to be setting up our tents shortly," said Mr. Harrod. "But first, we're all going to meet and learn some safety tips about campfires. Ready, ladies?"

Molly gulped, knowing that she had a few items to take care of before she could be around all those Scouts. "I'll be right there, Mr. Harrod."

He nodded and walked away with Mrs. Apple, Keiko and Felicia following. Molly heard a boy call out, "Hey, Mr. Harrod, didn't you say no pets on the camping trip?" and Mrs. Apple gave him the dirtiest look ever. Okay, not *the* dirtiest look;

that was reserved for the faces that Keiko and Felicia made at Molly as they walked away.

Molly grabbed her backpack and ran behind a tree with an enormous trunk. "Hey, guys, listen—" she started, gazing down at the tablet. Some grim faces gazed back up at her.

"I'm going to be straight with you, Molly," said Taffyta. "Those Shady Brook gals are trouble."

"With a capital *T*," agreed Snowanna.

Rancis held his hand up in solidarity. "You know I'm a fan of females, but the poison plant one scares me."

"They remind me of Sticky Wipplesnit and Torvald Batterbutter!" said Minty, her words rushing out. "They used to be Racers in *Sugar Rush*, but they kept running Jubileena Bing-Bing off the road into the Nesquik Sand Pit until finally King Candy put them on the Candy Cane Catapult and shot them out of the game!"

"Sweet mother of monkey milk, Minty," Vanellope said, exasperated. "Go back to rhyming, will ya?"

"Shmokay!" crowed Minty happily.

"Molly, I think you should give Kinko and Feldspar a chance," Vanellope continued, then turned to the other Racers. "Didn't we learn *any-thing* about the possibilities of friendship during the Sweet River Go-Kart Race?"

Taffyta sneered. "A dinky little race with your troop is not the same as being in the jungle with your enemy."

"It's not the jung—" Molly gave up, knowing

she would never convince Taffyta. "Listen, Racers, we need to keep you occupied. I think you should do your own Scavenger Hunt! You can look for items in all the games on my tablet."

This possibility actually distracted the Racers and they seemed excited, but then Snowanna raised her hand. "We were kind of arguing when you guys were talking about it on the bus, Molly, so remind us what a Scavenger Hunt is and then tell us every single rule."

"Oh, come on!" said Molly, feeling frantic.

"Gather 'round, Scouts!" Mr. Harrod bellowed from the campsite.

Molly knew she had less than thirty seconds to explain a Scavenger Hunt. "Okay! You separate into teams and the teams look for stuff—"

"Ooh!" Rancis's eyes lit up. "What stuff?"

Molly racked her brain, trying to remember what was said on the bus. "Uh, uh, some kind of cone—"

Minty tilted her head. "Bone?"

"Like, I don't know, like . . . an ice cream cone!"

Molly knew this didn't make sense, but she kept going. "And a feather . . . uh . . . duster. And something that starts with an *r*—something runny!" Molly cast a quick glance over at the campfire; it looked like every single Scout was there except her! So she kind of yelped the last item: "And something that makes a yellow noise!"

Molly quickly turned down the volume on the tablet and zipped her backpack shut, so quickly, in fact, that not one Racer got to ask the question that was on all of their minds:

"How can a noise be yellow?"

Chapter 5

"G oaterama!" squealed Minty.

The Racers were standing on the home screen of Molly's tablet, plotting out their very own Scavenger Hunt. Since they didn't have a coin, being game characters and all, they'd picked teams by flipping Rancis's peanut butter cup hat (he was not thrilled when it fell chocolate side down on Vanellope's dirty shoe). They ended up with Taffyta and Vanellope on one team, and Snowanna, Rancis, and Minty on the other. Choosing the video game each team was going to search *in* was proving to be much harder. Snowanna wanted her team to search for the Scavenger Hunt items in a game called—

"*Motor Mama*, Minty! Sheesh!" said Snowanna. Minty was her BFF, but this rhyming thing was straining their friendship more than the time

Minty knocked Snowanna's car off the racetrack into the Laffy Taffy Forest.

"'Goaterama,'" repeated Rancis, shaking his head. "Seriously, Minty? It sounds like we're doing our Scavenger Hunt on a sheep farm."

Vanellope was finishing up writing out the items to search for on two pieces of paper, her tongue sticking out from the effort. "Okay, my happy Hunters!" she crowed. "As you will see on my fabulous Scavenger Hunt list—"

"I can't even read this, Vanellope," said Taffyta, peering at the paper. "It looks like you wrote it with your toes instead of your fingers."

"—Our items are, as follows." Vanellope pretended she hadn't heard Taffyta and read from the list (squinting a little, since she actually couldn't read her writing, either). "An ice cream cone, a feather duster, something runny, and something that makes a yellow noise."

Rancis raised his hand.

"Yes, Rance?" said Vanellope.

"What's a feather duster?"

Vanellope scratched her chin with her pencil, leaving a mark. "Hmm. No idea. Just look for something that has feathers. And dust."

"I'm not touching anything runny," declared Taffyta.

Vanellope sighed and turned the pencil around to erase her chin mark. "Whatever, Taff."

"And I know which game we should do our Hunt in," Taffyta said.

"Oh, here it comes," mumbled Vanellope.

Taffyta marched across the screen, stomping her pink sneakers a little louder than was really necessary. At the very end, far away from the other game icons in a rather dark corner, she pointed to a rainbow icon that read CUTIE CARS AND CUDDLY CATS. "This one!"

"Nope," said Vanellope. "Nope, nope, nope."

Taffyta's bottom lip started to tremble. "Why not?" she said in her best everybody-is-against-me voice.

"Taff, you know the only reason that game is even on Molly's home screen is because you cried so hard she was afraid you were going to drown all of us and make the tablet malfunction," Vanellope said.

One single drop of mascara started down Taffyta's cheek. "Whatever a feather duster is, it would probably be around cuddly cats and not stinky cars!"

"Are ya looney? Cats are *way* stinkier than cars!" Vanellope said. "We're hunting in *Road Race Wrecker!*"

Taffyta wailed, and the tiny drop of mascara became a raging river down her cheek. "Teamwork makes the dream work!" (Except it sounded more like "dreee—eee—eam woooorrrrrkkkkk" because Taffyta was wailing.)

Snowanna raised her hand to ask a question. "Have we figured out what that means yet?"

"Nope," said Vanellope. "Nope, nope, nope."

"Soap, soap, soap," whispered Minty.

Rancis grabbed one of the lists out of Vanellope's hand. "We've got bigger problems than understanding a saying. We still haven't figured out what a yellow noise is."

"Holy hairy half of a ham sandwich, let's do this Hunt, people!" roared Vanellope, grabbing Taffyta's hand (which was a little damp from wiping away black tears) and dragging her to the *Road Race Wrecker* icon.

"And may the best team win!" Snowanna said, slinging her arms around Minty's and Rancis's shoulders.

"Bee boo skater!" Minty crowed.

And it was only because she waved wildly and blew kisses that the rest of the Racers understood that she meant, "See you later!"

Meanwhile, the Sweet River Outdoor Scouts were having a friendly little softball game before dinner with the Shady Brook Outdoor Scouts.

At least, it was *supposed* to be friendly.

Timmy and Tommy Lang were super annoyed with a boy in the Shady Brook troop named Derek Fitzsimmons. And though Molly's parents had taught her to find the good in every single person, even *she* found Derek rather annoying; he was just so full of himself! For instance:

"Do I have grass stains on my khaki shorts? They were very expensive," Derek asked after he sat on the ground for approximately three seconds at the meet'n'greet.

"Look how much bigger ours is than yours!" Derek said when the two troops were setting up their tents.

"I once wrestled a snake on a camping trip and saved my family from being poisoned," Derek bragged when they saw a teeny-weeny garter snake slither across their path.

And now, Rio was pitching in the softball game and Derek was coming up to bat, but instead of Timmy and Tommy (and pretty much everyone in the Sweet River troop) looking annoyed, the twins both sported huge grins. In the sunshine, their matching braces gleamed, and Molly looked at them suspiciously. What were they up to?

"New pitcher comin' in!" shouted Timmy and Tommy at the same time. For a moment, Molly wondered if both twins were going to take the pitcher's mound together, but only Tommy marched over, leaving Timmy snickering on first base. And for some reason, Tommy was carrying his own softball.

"Guess it's time we hit a homer," Derek said with a smirk, swinging his bat around and around for practice. Molly didn't doubt that Derek could hit a home run, since he was taller and looked stronger than the rest of the eleven-year-olds. But she really, really hoped he didn't, because she knew he would be bragging about it the whole weekend.

"Ready?" shouted Tommy (with Timmy shouting the same thing from first base).

"I was born ready!" Derek shouted back.

"Oh, brother," sighed Molly, but as it turned

out, she didn't have to worry about Derek bragging about anything. Because when Tommy pitched the ball and Derek hit it with his bat, super-duper hard, the ball didn't fly out for a homer.

In fact, it didn't fly at all.

It *exploded*.

Because it wasn't a ball at all, it was a giant *tomato* painted white to *look* like a ball.

"Aaarrgghhhfffeeemmyyy!" shrieked Derek as bright red juice, seeds, and tomato flesh burst all over his white T-shirt and expensive khaki shorts.

Molly gasped. The Sweet River troop started screaming and laughing, Timmy and Tommy the hardest (and the most coordinated). The Shady Brook troop, however, was not laughing; they were steaming mad. They gathered together and, glaring, faced the Sweet River troop, who quickly pulled themselves into a clump and glared back. The two troops were dead silent, staring and glaring.

"Hey! It looks just like *West Side Story*!" shouted a familiar voice.

Molly turned to see Jordan Jones, her new buddy, who usually hung out with the Sweet River girls' troop because he preferred their activities of volunteering, selling cookies, and doing musicals, of course. He'd obviously arrived late because he was still carrying all his gear, which he now dropped, gawking at Derek Fitzsimmons's tomato-covered face and body.

"It looks like *what*?" snarled Derek, wiping seeds from his eyes.

Jordan pulled himself together. "You never heard of the musical *West Side Story*?" he asked. "It's all about two gangs, the Jets and the Sharks, who don't like each other and fight for their turf."

"Well, that's perfect," said Rio, giving the other troop a look so dirty, it needed to wash its hands. "We'll be the Sweets and the Shades!"

"And we'll fight for our turf . . . with pranks!" said Timmy and Tommy.

Derek puffed out his chest, looking like a living and breathing spaghetti dinner. "Fine! But we warn you, we'll stop at nothing to get our revenge!" The Shades roared their approval.

"Us either! Vengeance!" echoed Rio. The Sweets roared back.

Jordan rolled his eyes at Molly with a grin, and she gave a little smile back. But as the two troops tried to top each other with roars, Molly's smile faded. It was *not* going to be pleasant sharing a tent tonight with the Shades.

Chapter
6

When Molly slipped into her sleeping bag that night, she was exhausted. They had done a whole day of cool camping stuff, like hiking, learning how to build a campfire, sitting by the lake (Timmy and Tommy had offered to jump into the frigid water for ten dollars but no one had any money, plus Mrs. Apple had given them a stern lecture about lake safety with Mortimer barking after every grim sentence), and more hiking. Even though Molly had discovered that hiking was basically the same as walking, it was way more fun to walk in the woods and over hills than to walk to school or, like, the dentist.

The day had been blissfully drama-free, but it had been quite an evening with the Battle of the Pranks (as Rio called it). At dinner, the Shades somehow snuck into the food supply and replaced all of the Sweets's burgers with mud patties and switched out the creamy centers of their Oreos with white toothpaste. So, yeah, *gross.*

By the time they had gotten to the campfire and spooky storytelling, both troops were cranky and the Sweets were hungry. There had been a short time of calm when Jordan Jones led them in campfire songs. They learned funny ones like "There's a Hole in the Bucket" and "Do Your Ears Hang Low?" Then one of the Sweets suggested "Goin' on a Bear Hunt," and just about the time they got to the lyric

Oh, look! It's a deep, dark cave,
Can't go under it, can't go over it,
Can't go through it, gotta go in it—

there was a bloodcurdling scream. "BEARS! *REAL* BEARS!" Felicia pointed into the trees, and it really did look like there were bears lurking there!

Of course, then everyone had gone running and screaming in every possible direction. Well, everyone except for Timmy and Tommy

Lang, who were busy holding flashlights with bear-shaped cutouts over the lenses and shining them into the woods to make it look like real bears were approaching. Molly had never seen Mr. Harrod lose his cool, but he was pretty mad about this prank (possibly because Mrs. Apple had fainted and fallen on him, knocking him off his comfy log seat, and Mortimer trotted over and stuck his tongue in Mr. Harrod's mouth).

By the time Mr. Harrod had revived Mrs. Apple, wiped his tongue with antiseptic, and gathered all the troops back together, it was super late and everyone was really tired. Molly was so pooped her eyes were closing all on their own, but she thought she'd better check in with the Racers before she conked out. She made sure to bury her head inside her sleeping bag and put her camp pillow over her face so Keiko and Felicia couldn't hear.

"Hey, guys," Molly whispered, "I just wanted to say good night—"

Suddenly, something bright pink and gooey splashed against the inside of the tablet screen, followed by a loud "Poops!" The voice was Minty's and she probably meant "Oops!," but Molly wasn't at all sure she wanted to know what the pink goo was, especially not right before she went to sleep.

The Racers popped out of their game icons and stared at the mess. "Well," Snowanna said,

"obviously, Minty found the ice cream cone, but since it melted, can we also say it was the 'something runny' on our Scavenger Hunt list?"

"No!" shrieked Taffyta. "That's cheating!"

"Sweet mother of strawberry monkey milk, Taff," said Vanellope, pointing to the bright pink blob, which was now dribbling sideways along the inside of the screen. "You gotta admit, that *is* runny."

Molly pulled the camp pillow tighter around her head. "Guys, a little quieter, please?!"

"Sorry, Molly," Rancis whispered, then sneezed about as loudly as a tiny game character can sneeze. All the Racers jumped about a mile, then turned to see Rancis holding up a handful of dirt with something poking out. "Sorry! I never figured out what a feather duster was, but I got dust and a feather. That counts, right?" He sneezed again, even louder than the first time.

A loud sniffling noise made Vanellope wheel around on Taffyta. "I swear, Taff, if I see one drop of mascara—"

But there wasn't any mascara, not even a drop. "I'm not crying, Vanellope. I do other things besides crying, you know," Taffyta said, her lower lip sticking out.

"Like pouting?" Minty said, trying to be helpful.

Taffyta sucked her lip back in.

Another loud sniffle made them all look around, then up at Molly. "Are we making you sad because we're too loud, Molly?" whispered Rancis, while making incredibly weird faces trying not to sneeze.

"I'm not crying, either," whispered Molly. She lifted one tiny smidgen of the camp pillow from her head and listened carefully.

Sniff.

The sound of crying wasn't coming from the tablet, it was coming from inside the tent.

"One of the Shades is crying!" whispered Molly.

The Racers got very worked up. "Who, who?" They quickly lifted Rancis, who wiped the strawberry ice cream goo from the screen with his sleeve, as Molly pulled the sleeping bag away from one eye. They all peered out.

Felicia was lying on top of her sleeping bag, sound asleep, snoring lightly through her stuffed-up allergy nose. That could only mean that the crier was—

"Keiko?" said Molly quietly. "Are you okay?"

More sniffling, and Keiko flipped over so that her back was to Molly and the Racers.

"Peas foamlick!" said Minty.

"She's homesick?" said Vanellope. "You really think so?"

Molly knew that her troop probably wouldn't be too happy if she tried to comfort the enemy, but she just couldn't help herself. "Keiko, are you foamlick—sorry, homesick?" Molly said, just a tiny bit louder.

Very, very slowly, Keiko turned back over and tried to give Molly a nasty side-eye, but it really didn't work with a tear sliding out of it. "So what if I am?" Keiko muttered. "What do you care?"

Molly was super tempted to say "I don't," but the truth was, she did.

And so did the Racers.

"Aw, we know what that feels like," whispered Rancis.

"Tell her it's gonna be okay!" whispered Snowanna.

"Everybody feels foamlick sometimes!" half rhyme-whispered Minty.

"It's okay to cry!" whispered Vanellope.

"Dang straight! Let it out, girl!" Taffyta yell-whispered, pumping her tiny fist. "Go ahead and wail, it feels awesome!"

Vanellope gave her a look. "You just gotta overdo it, don't you?"

Suddenly, Felicia woke up with a snorting, sneezing start. "What's happening?! Where am I?! Who put my bed outside?!"

Molly put her fingers to her lips to warn the Racers, then inched a smidgen out of her sleeping bag. "I think Keiko's feeling sad. Or maybe scared."

"Am not," said Keiko, but her voice squeaked on the "not."

Felicia shook her head to clear it. "Huh? Keiko's never sad. *Or* scared." She looked suspiciously at Molly. "What did you do to her?!"

Molly didn't exactly *hear* the Racers object to this accusation, but the tablet started to tremble with rage. Fearing a loud outburst of "How dare you!" that would freak Keiko and Felicia out even further, Molly quickly opened her mouth to defend herself. But as it turned out, she didn't have to.

"Molly didn't do anything," Keiko admitted. "I *am* sad, Felicia. And maybe a little bit scared, too." She sniffled.

Felicia's mouth dropped open in shock. Then she dug around in her sleeping bag and produced a wad of tissues, leaning over to Keiko. "They're snot-free," she whispered.

Keiko made a face, but wiped her eyes with the tissues.

"Molly," a tiny voice hissed from the depths of

her sleeping bag. "Tell her about how I cried on Butcher Boy's meaty shoulder after I left *Sugar Rush* to live in *Slaughter Race*."

Felicia turned to look at Molly. "Did you say something?"

"Uh, uh," fumbled Molly. "Sometimes I kind of mumble to myself when I'm trying to figure out how to help someone."

"O-*kay*," said Felicia, obviously not convinced.

"Yeah, I, uh . . ." Molly dug back into her memory to produce an explanation. "I was reminding myself about the time I cried on my grandpa's meaty shoulder—*sorry*, just a regular shoulder—when I went and stayed with my grandparents for the summer. I was happy to be there, but I missed my home, too. I felt both things at the same time."

Now it was Keiko's mouth that dropped open, and she half sat up. "That's exactly how *I* feel. I'm really excited to be here, but I really miss my family and my house, too."

"And that's fine!" said Molly (a little louder than necessary, because she was trying to cover up Snowanna launching into a monologue about how much she really loved Molly, but she also missed having dance parties with Adorabeezle back in *Sugar Rush*). "And if you need to cry some more, we can sit here with you."

Keiko did a long, rather moist sniffle and fixed Molly with a stare that almost looked friendly. *Almost.* "You're okay, Molly. Ya know, for being the enemy and all."

"Yeah, you're like, almost *nice*," said Felicia.

"Well, thanks." Molly smiled.

There was a slightly awkward pause, which Keiko broke with a yawn. "I think I can sleep now. 'Night." She turned her back to Molly, but this time it wasn't a mean back. Felicia gave Molly a little nod, then lay back down. In a moment, she was making all sorts of weird sleep noises through her stuffed-up nose.

Molly breathed a huge sigh of relief and

snuggled down into her sleeping bag. The Racers looked up at her with some admiration.

"Wood snob, Lolly," said Minty.

This one took Molly a moment. "Is that 'good job'?"

Minty nodded, grinning.

"Well, this has all been supersweet and inspiring and whatnot," said Vanellope. "But there's still something we have to figure out." She flung her hands up to the sky as if asking the video-game gods this eternal question: "Where the *heck* are we gonna find a yellow noise?!"

Chapter 7

When Molly, Keiko, and Felicia came out of their tent the next morning and walked together to the central fire pit for breakfast, Scouts from both troops glared at them. Mr. Harrod and Mrs. Apple didn't look much happier; they both had dark circles under their eyes and were chugging coffee made in a little pot set over the flames. Mortimer was lying on his back inside Mrs. Apple's huge, ugly handbag, snoring a huge, ugly snore.

Molly spotted Rio and sidled over to him. "What's going on? Everybody's looking super cranky."

"Seriously? You didn't hear all the yelling in the middle of the night?" Rio asked.

"What?! No!" said Molly, surprised. But then she thought about it and realized that the Racers had been driving all night in search of a yellow noise and the sounds of their cars might have drowned anything else out, especially since Molly had slept zipped up tightly inside her sleeping bag.

"The Shades pulled a nasty prank," Rio said, making a face. "They drew spiders on the toilet paper in the outhouse."

"Ooh, that is nasty," said Molly, shuddering at the thought.

"Yeah, well, Mr. Harrod and Mrs. Apple are pretty ticked off," said Rio. "Who knows what they're going to say at breakfast?"

They didn't have to wait long to find out, because just at that moment, Mr. Harrod pulled out a whistle and blew on it—hard. All the Scouts jumped and quickly came to the fire pit, where Mrs. Apple stood up, her face even redder than usual.

"First of all, campers," she began, "this morning is breakfast-in-a-bag." Mrs. Apple pointed to a stack of brown paper bags. "One slice of bacon, one egg, and a handful of cheese goes in each bag; hang it on a stick, and cook it over the fire."

"But I'm a vegetarian—" started one of the Shades.

"Silence!" Mrs. Apple roared.

Everyone silenced, except for Mortimer, who woke up with an irritated snort-bark. Mrs. Apple took a deep breath, and a long sip of coffee, and arranged a smile on her round face. "Sorry, just a mite crabby this morning *since I only got about an hour of sleep.*" Her smile slipped a bit as the Shades gulped. "But that's fine, because we've made a plan—isn't that right, Mr. Harrod?"

Now Mr. Harrod stood. "That's right, we've made a p-p-puh—" He couldn't quite get it out because he was yawning.

"A p-p-puh-plan?" someone called out. There were a few scattered giggles that stopped immediately when Mrs. Apple's mouth set in a straight line and Mortimer growled.

"Today's Scavenger Hunt is going to be a little different," announced Mrs. Apple. "Usually, it's one troop competing against another. But we feel there's been enough competition on this camping trip, isn't that right, Mr. Harrod?"

"That is correct, Mrs. Apple, there has been competition galore," said Mr. Harrod drily. "Therefore! We are going to mix the troops together and make several teams with members of both troops in each team."

A howl went up among the campers.

"That's not fair!" howled the Shades.

"That's *totally* not fair!" howled the Sweets.

Mr. Harrod blew his whistle again, and everyone quieted down. "You have two choices: mixed teams or no Scavenger Hunt at all. Your troop leaders have spoken." He took a slug of his coffee and sat down hard on his log, teetering a bit.

"Line up for breakfast-in-a-bag!" said Mrs. Apple.

The two troops lined up, but you never heard more grumbling and muttering. They griped when they opened their brown paper bags, moaned when they put in a slice of bacon, fussed over the cheese, sniveled when they cracked an egg into the bag, and whined when they hung the bags on roasting sticks. It was the whining that finally got to Molly; she hated whining.

"Guys, seriously," Molly said to her troop as she folded the edges of her bag over her stick. "Is this really such a big deal? The Scavenger Hunt will still be fun."

The Sweets looked at Molly like she'd grown a second head. And speaking of matching heads—

"Are you cray-cray?" said Timmy and Tommy Lang, perfectly in unison, as usual. "The Hunt is *ruined*! This is a *disaster*!"

"But why?" Molly said. "I don't think the Shades are all that bad. Keiko and Felicia are pretty nice, actually."

The Sweets gasped in shock. Timmy's and Tommy's faces turned so purple from anger, the whites of their eyes seemed to glow.

Molly was about to explain, but Rio quickly interrupted. "Don't freak out, guys. Remember, Molly is new to our troop and she doesn't know what the Shades are capable of. She doesn't understand how low-down and nasty they can be."

Molly put her hands on her hips, a little annoyed at her bestie. "First of all, I can speak for myself, Rio. And secondly, *we've* been pretty low-down and nasty, too."

"Yeah, but—" Rio started.

"Less talking, more roasting!" called out Mr. Harrod. He was still sitting on the log, his eyes now closed. But not his ears, obviously.

The troops moved to the fire, and as they hung their bags over the flames to cook the breakfast inside, there was no sound. Just a whole bunch of glaring, pouting, and sneering. That is, until—

"AAAAHHH!" Keiko shrieked as her brown paper bag slipped off the roasting stick and fell into the fire. It burned rapidly, popping and sizzling from the greasy bacon.

As the Sweets started to snicker and comment, Molly turned her roasting stick around quickly and tried to pull Keiko's bag out of the flames with the other end. Of course, Mrs. Apple and Mortimer happened to walk up at that exact moment, and Derek Fitzsimmons seized the opportunity.

"Molly knocked Keiko's bag into the fire!" he yelled.

"What?! I did not!" Molly said, but her voice was drowned out by the Shades' shouts of agreement, the Sweets' shouts of anger, and Mortimer's indignant barking.

"Hold on, hold on, all of you," said Mr. Harrod. He forced his eyes open and rose stiffly from his log, walking over with one hand on his aching back. "Keiko, what happened?"

Keiko looked around nervously at her troop, who were glaring back at her with narrowed eyes. "Uh . . ."

"She turned away for a second and Molly whacked Keiko's bag with her stick!" said Derek Fitzsimmons, pointing to Molly's roasting stick. "You can see it right in front of you!"

"I was trying to get it *out* of the fire!" said Molly. "Keiko, tell them!"

But Keiko gulped and looked down at her feet.

Molly turned to Felicia. "Felicia, you saw what happened!"

But Felicia gulped and looked down at her packet of tissues.

"All right, let's just move on from this," said Mr. Harrod, sighing.

"But—" Derek Fitzsimmons started to object.

"*Move on,*" said Mrs. Apple, and her voice

made it very clear that moving on would be the only path forward. She picked Mortimer up and flounced back to her seat.

But Molly found that she couldn't move on. As she turned her stick around to cook her breakfast-in-a-bag, she muttered, "Of all the low-down, nasty—" She caught Rio's eye, and he nodded. Molly nodded back.

The Shades really *were* the enemy.

"I will not surrender to the enemy!" shouted Taffyta, thrusting her lollipop above her head like a sword.

"Shmenemy?" repeated Minty, looking with confusion at Snowanna and Rancis. They both just shook their heads and sat down wearily on the home screen.

"Sweet soft-serve on a sideways snake, Taff," sighed Vanellope. She was lying on her back in a dark corner of the home screen, and all the other

Racers could see were her shoes. Well, one foot with a shoe and one foot with only a sock, and the sock had a hole through which her big toe stuck out. "For the last time, Minty, Snow, and Rance are not the enemy. It was supposed to be a friendly game."

"A friendly game that we'll never, ever finish," moaned Rancis, hugging his peanut butter cup to his chest. "Because we'll never, ever find a yellow noise."

"I found out what 'scavenger' actually means," said Snowanna, whose snow hair was melting from heat exhaustion. "It's an animal that eats other animals. Dead ones."

"Well thanks, Snow, for that un-fun fact," said Vanellope. "Taffyta, if neither team can find the last Scavenger Hunt item, we'll have to quit."

"Quit?! The Muttonfudges never quit!" Taffyta thundered, rising to her pink tippy toes.

The other four Racers groaned.

"Well, our team is *not* going back into *Motor Mama*, I'm telling you now," said Snowanna. "One of those crazy mamas rode her motorcycle right over me." She turned around, and sure enough, there was a tire track across her purple back.

"*Road Race Wrecker* was pretty rough, too," admitted Vanellope. She wiggled her big toe. "I think I lost my shoe on the Gear Grinder Gateway."

"Ouch," said the Racers.

Rancis plopped the peanut butter cup hat back on his head in frustration, totally flattening the one golden curl in his hair. "So, do we just tell Molly that we couldn't finish the Scavenger Hunt? Seems pretty sad. What are we gonna do, guys?"

Suddenly, Minty leapt to her feet, excited. "Reem flerk!"

The Racers looked at her blankly.

"Not even trying to guess that one," Snowanna said.

As pooped as Vanellope was, she couldn't resist giving it a shot. "Beam ... cream ... deem ... Oh, I know! Meme jerk!"

Now they all looked at Vanellope blankly.

"Yeah, you're right, that's not a thing," she said, continuing to rhyme. "Seem ... team ..." Now Vanellope leapt to her feet, almost slipping on that one sock. "I got it! *Teamwork*!"

Minty clapped happily while Taffyta made a gagging face. "I like 'meme jerk' better."

"Now, what did Molly's dad say in the tent store ..." Vanellope said as she started pacing, tapping a tiny finger on her teeny-tiny lip. "You use the strengths of each person to accomplish the big goal, right? What if we figured out our strengths and then found this yellow noise together as one team?!"

"Yes, yes!" Rancis leapt to his feet.

"I know my strength!" said Snowanna, some of her energy returning. "I'm all about the music, y'all!" She started to dance, stomping her groovy purple boots.

"Mine is definitely my superstrong muscles!" said Rancis, showing off one of his measly biceps. "Right?"

"Mmm . . ." murmured Vanellope.

Minty shook her head and pointed at Rancis. "Meat."

"Well, thank you, Minty!" Rancis said with a smile and struck another muscle-y pose.

"I think she means 'sweet,' Rance," said Snowanna.

Rancis sighed and dropped his not-really-that-superstrong arm. "Okay. I guess 'sweet' is a good strength."

Vanellope continued to pace, her one exposed toe skidding on the floor. "We all know Minty's strength is—"

"Sliming!" Minty yelped.

"Yeah, rhyming, we know—" Vanellope said.

"And offering totally helpful suggestions all the time," continued Minty, dropping her rhyming long enough to get a few more "strengths" in.

"Well . . ." Snowanna and Rancis looked at each other with hesitation.

"Oh! And telling great stories about our days in *Sugar Rush*," Minty said, rubbing her tiny hands together in glee. "Tales full of drama and adventure and candy crime and good gumballs gone bad—"

"Okay, simmer down, Mint," Vanellope said, patting her shoulder. "Now, *my* strength is obviously being the brains of the group."

"Um, *excuse* me?" interrupted Taffyta, finally lowering her lollipop and rubbing her sore shoulder. "If you're the brains, then what's my strength?"

"Frying?" suggested Minty.

"Crying *is* one of Taffyta's strengths, Mint," said Vanellope. "But I don't know if it's gonna help us much for this."

"Being difficult?" suggested Snowanna.

"Well, yeah, but let's not be mean—" mused Vanellope.

"Always being the last one to agree to anything so we all have to wait and beg and plead for her to change her mind?" interrupted Rancis.

"Okay, Taffyta *is* very good at that," agreed Vanellope.

"Oh, hold on just a sugar-licking minute," said Taffyta, a grin sliding across her face. "I know *exactly* what my strength is."

"What?" asked the Racers.

"All of the above!" crowed Taffyta. Then, as if by magic, her eyes filled with tears and mascara started sliding down her face as she wailed, "I'll only join in if we search for the yellow noise in *Cutie Cars and Cuddly Cats*! It's the only place we haven't looked yet! You know I'm right! I'll just wait here!" She stamped her foot, crossed her arms, and, yes, waited for the begging and pleading.

The Racers all looked at each other.

"She really is good at that," sighed Rancis.

"Floatally," agreed Minty.

Molly wasn't sure if Derek Fitzsimmons was wearing his tomato-stained T-shirt because it was the only shirt he'd brought, or because he wanted to remind the Sweets that the Prank War was still on. Either way, Molly was able to see—and smell—that tomato-y mess up close because . . .

Derek Fitzsimmons was on her Scavenger Hunt team.

And so were Keiko and Felicia, looking about as friendly as a pair of hornets who just had their nest kicked.

And so were Timmy and Tommy Lang, who were quivering with rage in perfectly synchronized vibrations.

"This is a disaster," Molly whispered to Rio, who luckily got switched to their team at the last minute, keeping it from being a *total* disaster.

"I know," Rio whispered back. "Do you think they'll try to push us off a cliff or something?"

"Probably just cover us in honey and leave us for the bears," grumbled Molly.

"SCOUTS!" bellowed Mr. Harrod, whose strong voice and eyelids that remained open showed that he'd obviously taken a nap after breakfast. "The Scavenger Hunt teams have been chosen, and they're written in stone!"

"Huh?" questioned one of the Shades.

Mrs. Apple leaned wearily against a tree as Mortimer licked her exposed ankle. "It just means you can't change the teams around, kid. You've never heard that expression before? Sheesh." Obviously, Mrs. Apple had *not* taken a nap after breakfast.

"You have fifteen minutes to go to your tents and grab your backpacks and water bottles and meet back here!" shouted Mr. Harrod. The campers turned to go. "AND—" Mr. Harrod continued, with as stern a voice as he could manage, being a pretty nice guy and all. "You're all going to shake hands before you head out to the Hunt!"

"Only if no one's touched poison ivy," muttered Keiko, looking miserable.

"Grrrr," Molly growled. This was seriously a nightmare. She could only hope the Racers were having more fun on their Scavenger Hunt than she was about to have on hers.

"Farting felines on a furry frankfurter!" shouted Vanellope. "Can we please get out of here now?"

"But they're so adorbs!" cried Taffyta.

Vanellope made a face of disgust.

There were cats *everywhere*. Orange cats were swirling around the Racers' feet, creamy white cats were climbing up their legs, striped cats were clinging to their shoulders, and rainbow-colored cats were nestling on their heads. Rancis had been trying to shake a bright green cat out of his peanut butter cup hat for half an hour and there

was a fluorescent perched on Snowanna's shoulder, looking quite comfortable she was pretty sure it was coming back to *Sugar Rush* with her. Even Minty wasn't rhyming much, since there was a cat wrapped around her neck like a scarf with its tail covering her mouth.

"How come there's more cats than cars?" grumbled Vanellope, trying to escape a polka-dotted kitten who was batting her exposed toe with his paws. "Isn't this supposed to be *Cutie Cars and Cuddly Cats*? The title says 'Cars' first!"

Taffyta pointed with her lollipop. "There's a cutie car right over there!"

"Where? All I see are more cats," said Vanellope, peering at what looked like a moving mountain of furry tails and bouncy whiskers.

"The car is *under* the cats, silly!" Taffyta giggled.

"Okay, that's it!" Vanellope yelped. "We found our yellow noise, time to go!"

And it was true; with teamwork, the Racers *had* found their yellow noise. It was a song called

"Here Comes the Super Sunny Sun!" and—you guessed it—it was the theme song of *Cutie Cars and Cuddly Cats*. It even had a line that went, *"The summertime is super fun, a yellow noise comes from the sun!"*

"It's so . . . perky. And it just keeps playing . . . and playing . . ." said Rancis, dazed.

Vanellope clapped her hands in front of his face. "Snap out of it, Rance!"

"Mmmfffggggzzz," mumbled Minty, her eyes huge and staring.

Vanellope pulled the cat's tail away from her mouth. "What's that, Mint?"

Minty spat out some fur and whispered, "Slow. Bore. Fats."

"I agree, Minty. No more cats." Vanellope unwrapped the extra-long feline from Minty's neck and chucked it into the pile on the cutie car. "We're outta here!"

The Racers waded through the knee-deep piles of meowers and made it to the exit of *Cutie Cars and Cuddly Cats*, pausing for a moment at the end to help Snowanna remove the fluorescent kitten from her shoulder. They hopped back onto the home screen, and as they brushed fur off each other, Vanellope noticed something concerning.

"Electrical eels on the edge of eternity!" she exclaimed, pointing to a symbol next to the volume buttons. "Look at how low Molly's battery is!"

The Racers looked. The little battery symbol was red instead of green!

"Twenty percent!" said Snowanna.

Rancis grimaced. "Yikes. I guess we should have thought about there being nowhere to recharge."

"Ooh! Ooh! I know!" exclaimed Minty, who was occasionally putting aside her strength for rhyming to use her strength for offering helpful suggestions. "If there's a storm tonight, Molly can put her tablet outside so it gets struck by lightning! That'll charge it right up!"

"Um, pretty sure that would fry the tablet, Minty," said Rancis.

Snowanna grimaced. "Barbecued Racers."

"You guys, this is no biggie," said Taffyta, flicking her wrist. "Just tell Molly to power down. We can take a delicious nap in the Cloud and wake up when it's time to leave the jungle and return to civilization."

"Bungle?" asked Minty.

Vanellope looked perturbed, but the Racers weren't quite sure if it was because of Taffyta or because she was still finding cat hair in weird places on her body. "I hate it when you're right, Taff, but when you're right, you're right."

"You say that like sometimes I'm *not* right," said Taffyta, her eyebrows rising.

"GUYS!" Molly's face appeared above them so suddenly that Rancis screamed a little (then pretended he was coughing). "You're not gonna believe this! I'm on a Scavenger Hunt team with, like, a million Shades!"

"No!" gasped Snowanna.

"YES!" Molly knew she was being extra loud, but this was worthy of a good yell, right? "And

Keiko and Felicia are being super nasty now, like last night never even happened!"

"Golly. Wowza. How awful." Taffyta yawned. "So, like, we need a nap—"

"—Kin! We need a nap*kin*, Molly!" Vanellope broke in. "Um, um . . . Taffyta ate some of that runny ice cream and dribbled all over her chin!"

The Racers looked at Vanellope in complete confusion, and Taffyta was downright horrified. "Ex*cuse* me? The Muttonfudges do not dribble!"

Molly was pretty lost herself. "Uh . . . I think we've figured out that I can't really give you things through my device, Vanellope. 'Cause there's a screen between us and all."

"Ohhhh, silly me on a sideways flea!" chuckled Vanellope manically, pinching Taffyta hard on her arm as she kept trying to interrupt. "Just get yourself ready for the Hunt, Moll; don't worry about us sloppy kids!"

"O-*kay*," said Molly, still mystified. But she *did* need to get her water bottle and bug spray and stuff to go on this miserable, awful, terrible Scavenger Hunt, so with a tremendous sigh, she dropped her backpack and went to collect her things.

Which is exactly what Vanellope was hoping for. "Racers! I know I said Taffyta was right when she wanted to power down the tablet—"

"I *was* right and *stop pinching me!*" hissed Taffyta. Vanellope released her arm, and Taffyta kissed her own boo-boos noisily.

"But we *have* to be with Molly on this Scavenger

Hunt!" Vanellope whispered intensely. "We can't leave her alone with the evil Shades, *especially* not with Keychain and Falafel!"

Minty's forehead crinkled. "Do you mean Keiko and Fel—"

Rancis interrupted, lifting one superstrong arm in protest. "Vanellope's right! We have to be with Molly!"

Snowanna jumped up to peer out of the tablet (and bonked her head on the screen, but crunchy cushioning is one of the benefits of having a snow cone for hair). "Her backpack is open! That means it's time for—"

"Reem flerk!" Minty gasped.

And the Racers didn't even correct her rhyming, because "reem flerk makes the dream work," or at least *this* time it did. All the Racers ran toward the side of the tablet in perfect rhythm— even Timmy and Tommy Lang would have been proud—and slammed into it, sending the tablet flying off the camp chair and right smack into Molly's open backpack. They were a little

nervous that Molly would hear them, so they muffled their "Wheeees!" and "Whooaahhs!" but lucky for the Racers, Mr. Harrod blew his whistle outside. Molly just grabbed her backpack and ran, not even noticing that there were now five colorful helpers prepped and ready to do whatever it took to protect Molly from the enemy.

That is, of course, as long as a battery on twenty percent power would allow them to.

Chapter 9

Jordan Jones waved cheerfully at Molly from across the campfire circle. She managed a wave back, but the truth was, she was super jelly of how excited Jordan's Scavenger Hunt group looked. They were singing show tunes so happily that Molly saw one boy from her troop crack a *smile*, for the love of Pete!

It sure was different on Molly's side of the campfire circle. Derek Fitzsimmons had finally changed, thank goodness, because Molly had been having nightmares about a bird swooping down to eat Derek's tomato-stained shirt right in the middle of the Hunt. But Derek *hadn't* changed his facial expression, which was a combination of snooty, sour, and suspicious. Keiko and Felicia stood on either side of him with three expressions of their own: unfriendly, *super* unfriendly, and totally ignoring anyone who might *be* friendly. Keiko had her nose buried in a guidebook about identifying poisonous plants, and Felicia had *her* nose wedged with tissues, but she kept sneezing them right out of her nostrils. It was not a pretty sight.

Timmy and Tommy stood closer to Molly and Rio, not too close, of course, but close enough that Molly could hear them grumbling in unison: "Can't believe we have to be with *them*. We're totally gonna lose because of *them*. We'll probably get eaten by a mountain lion because of *them*."

"I suppose that's better than getting pushed off a cliff," mumbled Rio.

A loud, shrill whistle brought everyone to attention. Mr. Harrod and Mrs. Apple walked to the center of the grumpy Scavenger Hunt teams and motioned for them to move closer. Nobody did, because they didn't *want* to be any closer to each other. Mr. Harrod opened his mouth to speak, but before he could get one word out—

"I have a suggestion!" Derek Fitzsimmons called out.

All the Outdoor Scouts groaned. Even Mr. Harrod and Mrs. Apple groaned, although they did it with very little sound as they were trying to be an example and not be annoyed at the annoying Derek Fitzsimmons. But Molly could have sworn she saw Mortimer roll his large, googly eyes.

"Before we start the Scavenger Hunt, I propose that Mr. Harrod and Mrs. Apple check every single camper," said Derek in his usual snooty "I'm smarter than you" voice. He walked a bit closer to Molly. "We need to make sure no one is carrying any suspicious prank materials in their backpacks."

While more groaning happened among the teams, Molly breathed a giant sigh of relief that she'd left her tablet in the tent and *not* in her backpack.

Of course, inside her backpack on the tablet that was *not* in the tent, there was a slightly different reaction.

"WE'RE BUSTED!" shrieked Taffyta.

"Noisy Nellie on a Nerfball, Taff!" hissed Vanellope. "Do you have to scream?!"

"Snide!" yelped Minty, looking around for a game icon to jump into and hide. Snowanna and Rancis started running wildly from one end of the tablet to the other, bumping into each other at every turn.

"It's not going to help us to hide, guys!" said Vanellope, exasperated. "Unless you can figure out a way to make the whole tablet go invisible!"

Taffyta fell to her knees, her short, stubby arms in the air, drama oozing from every pore. "We'll be confiscated and imprisoned in Mrs. Apple's ugly handbag! We'll be eaten by Mortimer, digested, and pooped out in a suburban yard! We'll never make it back to Litwak's!"

"Pitsnack's!" howled Minty.

And the situation looked dire indeed, as Mr. Harrod slowly approached Derek Fitzsimmons and Molly. He got . . .

Closer . . . (The Racers shook in their groovy boots.)

Closer . . . (Taffyta fainted, and Rancis melted into a Rancis-puddle.)

Closer . . . (Snowanna started singing *Farewell, Fun Dip* in a very sad voice.)

Right next to Molly, Mr. Harrod reached his hand out toward the backpack and . . . *past* it . . . to pat Derek Fitzsimmons on the shoulder. "Young man, it's time we all decided to trust one another, don't you think?"

Derek's snooty face fell. He mumbled, "I guess so," but it wasn't very convincing.

Inside the backpack, Vanellope breathed a huge sigh of relief while Snowanna switched to singing *One More Chance (for a Charleston Chew)* in a happy voice, Minty helped Rancis up from his Rancis-puddle, and they *were* going to wake Taffyta up from her faint, but she said she needed a nap, right?

"Scavenger Hunt lists!" called out Mrs. Apple

in a shrill voice, pulling a stack of papers from inside her giant ugly handbag. The campers passed the lists around, being careful not to touch anyone from the "enemy" side (which was pretty much everyone), and looked at Mrs. Apple's fancy writing:

1. *Something fuzzy*
2. *A pine cone*
3. *Something rough*
4. *A bug*
5. *A mud-covered stick*
6. *Animal poop (no need to bring this one back, just for observation)*

Of course, everyone went ballistic over the last item, but amidst all the noise, Molly actually laughed a little. "Ohhh, *pine* cone! That's what it was! I can't believe I told them to find an *ice cream* cone."

"Told who?" said Rio, reading the list over her shoulder.

Molly froze. "Uhh . . ." She thought fast. "I, uh, had a dream that the Racers wanted to do their own Scavenger Hunt."

"Ooof," said Rio. "Can you imagine the Racers on a Hunt? They're so competitive, it would be more of a *nightmare* than a dream!" He laughed heartily.

Inside the backpack, the Racers looked at each other.

"Should we be insulted?" asked Rancis.

"Nah," said Vanellope with a grin. "Our boy knows us!"

Minty giggled. "Frightsquare!"

"But a *fun* nightmare!" Snowanna said, laughing.

Taffyta said nothing. She was still out cold on the home screen.

Outside the backpack, Derek Fitzsimmons was saying to anyone who would listen, "I'm telling you, someone is gonna prank us with plastic dog poop!" But no one was really listening. They were too busy talking about how happy/mad they were that they didn't have to actually *touch* the animal doodoo and whether you had to find the stick already muddy or if you could just put mud *on* a stick and—

The whistle blew! "Campers! Start your Hunt!" shouted Mr. Harrod.

"What he said," echoed Mrs. Apple, who looked like she was fully ready to go back home and sleep in her own bed. "Oh, and don't forget to have one person from each team take a trail map." She pointed an elbow at her ugly handbag, because pointing a finger is exhausting.

Someone from each team ran over and grabbed a map (they had to move Mortimer, who had plopped his chubby butt and corkscrew tail on the papers). Then the teams all took off in different directions.

The Scavenger Hunt had begun!

Chapter 10

. . . **A**nd tree bark is *not* rough enough to qualify as 'something rough,' unless it's a white ash tree, which has triangle-shaped furrows—" Derek Fitzsimmons had been talking since they left the campfire circle.

"*Duh*, the white ash has *diamond*-shaped furrows and they're totes rough—" And Keiko had been arguing with him just as long.

"Do we have to bring back a live bug, or can it be dead?" Felicia had asked this question at least a hundred times. Molly was pretty sure the answer Felicia wanted was "dead."

"Can't believe we're stuck with *them*," mumbled Timmy and Tommy Lang in perfect unison, over and over again until Molly felt like her head was going to explode. It was such a beautiful day and she was trying to enjoy it, but the arguing was making Molly feel like maybe her mother was right; all vacations should be at nice hotels with heated swimming pools.

As their Scavenger Hunt team marched and marched and marched some more through the woods, they discussed (fought over) every single item on the list, including whether a pine *cone* had to come from a pine *tree* and just how fuzzy "something fuzzy" had to be. Molly had found a fuzzy caterpillar, but they couldn't all agree if it was fuzzy enough, because Felicia couldn't bring herself to look at it, and *nobody* could bring themselves to look at the rabbit droppings Rio discovered.

But it wasn't very long before they realized they had bigger problems than poo viewing.

"Hey, guys, the trail splits in two here," said Molly, pointing to the paths and trying to raise her voice over the fights. "Which way are we supposed to go?"

Timmy and Tommy rolled their eyes, and both sets landed in a perfect, irritated side-eye focused right on Molly. "Look at the map. Sheesh."

Rio rolled his eyes back at them with such force it almost equaled their double-roll. "Who *has* the map? Sheesh."

They all stopped walking (and arguing) and looked at each other.

Silence.

"Come on, guys," said Molly. "Who from our team went over and took the trail map from Mrs. Apple's ugly purse?"

They all looked at each other again. Only this time the look was kind of nervous.

"Nobody took the trail map from the ugly purse?" whispered Felicia.

They all looked at each other again. Only this time the look was sheer panic.

"WE'RE LOST!" shrieked Timmy and Tommy, but they weren't as coordinated as usual, so it sounded kind of echo-y, like "WE'RE—E'RE LOST—OST!" Keiko turned white. Felicia whimpered and zipped her jacket up over her face, presumably so no bugs would eat her.

Rio tried to remain calm. "We're not lost! All we have to do is turn around and follow this trail back to camp."

"Except . . ." said Molly, cringing a little. "There were parts where there *was* no trail, we were just walking on the grass. And a couple of times there were other splits in the trail and we just kept randomly walking."

Keiko's mouth made a little *o*. "What?! Why didn't you say anything?!"

"Because I couldn't even get a word in!" exclaimed Molly. "Because you and Derek were fighting about everything!"

They all turned toward Derek Fitzsimmons. But to their surprise, he *laughed*. "You people think I didn't plan ahead for something like this? I *always* plan ahead." He pulled a bag of popcorn from his backpack with his usual snooty grin. "I've been dropping these as we walked! So all we have to do is follow them back to camp."

Timmy and Tommy looked at him with grudging admiration. Felicia unzipped her jacket just far enough to say thanks. Color came back to Keiko's face. Even Rio held out his hand for a fist bump.

But Molly had a weird expression on her face. "Um . . . guys?" She pointed.

A fat little squirrel—extra fat, for reasons suddenly becoming painfully clear—sat on the trail behind them, nibbling on a piece of popcorn and staring at them as if to say *More, please.*

The Scavenger Hunt team stared back. Then looked past the fat squirrel at the trail, which was dusty and dirty and trail-like, but also empty. Of popcorn, that is. There were other, *ahem*, things strewn along the path.

"Well . . ." said Rio. "At least we know where to spy some animal poop now . . ."

"WE'RE GOING TO HAVE TO LIVE THE REST OF OUR LIVES IN THIS JUNGLE!!" shrieked Taffyta. It was fairly impressive, considering that she had just woken up from her faint and was still lying on the home screen.

Vanellope put her tiny hands on her tiny hips. "For real, Taff? First thing out of your mouth?"

"All we have to do is let Molly know we're in

her backpack!" said Rancis, rushing over to an icon and pointing. "Because, look!"

"G . . . P . . . S . . ." said Snowanna. "Gooey Peanut S'mores?"

"No—"

"Gummy Peppermint Sugarbombs?" Snowanna tried again.

"Can you stop!"

"Galactic Pushpop Sweet Tarts?"

"SNOWANNA!" the Racers shouted.

Minty sighed happily. "I love when someone else gets yelled at besides me."

"A GPS is for directions, Snow," said Vanellope. "I had one on my car in *Slaughter Race*, so I could always find my way home and avoid all the flaming dumpster fires and vicious land sharks."

Taffyta eyed Vanellope from the ground. "I'm gonna ask it again—*why* did you leave *Sugar Rush*?"

Vanellope ignored this. "What do you think, Racers? If we alert Molly to our presence, she could use the GPS to find their way back to camp.

But when they find out she brought an electronic device on the trip, she could get in big fat trouble."

"Pig rat bubble..." mused Minty, then shook her head.

"Oof," grimaced Snowanna. "What if she gets kicked out of the Outdoor Scouts and it's all our fault?"

Taffyta, who was now on her feet and re-sucking her lollipop, said, "Well, you know what's worse than getting in big fat trouble?"

"What?" asked Rancis and Snowanna. (It was only Rancis and Snowanna because Minty said, "Butt?" and Vanellope said, "*Please* don't ask 'what,' guys.")

"LIVING THE REST OF OUR LIVES IN THIS JUNGLE!" Taffyta shrieked.

Vanellope put a finger in her ear and jiggled it. "Even though you owe me a new eardrum, Taff, you've got a point. But in order to get her attention, we're gonna need a little—"

"Reem flerk!" cried Minty.

Vanellope nodded. "On the count of three, guys . . ."

After a couple of false starts (because Rancis insisted that you count one-two-three and *then* shout, but Taffyta insisted you shout *on* three, and Minty kept saying bun-poo-pee and giggling), they finally did it.

"MOLLY!!!"

Chapter 11

And it worked, because *everyone* heard it.

"Um . . ." said Keiko hesitantly. "Is your backpack . . . yelling?"

Rio whispered out of the side of his mouth, "What the heck, Moll? Did you bring them and not tell me?!"

Her face turning bright red, Molly was just about to stick her head into her bag and give the Racers a piece of her mind, when another shout made her think twice.

"G! P! S!"

"Oh! OH!" Molly's eyes brightened. "Right! Uh, excuse me for a sec, this might look weird, but I can explain—" Yeah, there was no explanation that was going to make this *not* weird. So, she just went ahead and stuck her head into her bag. "Guys, hide, okay?"

Vanellope saluted. "Aye, aye, Captain Crush-It!" The Racers scattered and hid behind icons on the home screen, and Molly pulled the tablet out of her backpack.

"Guys, I have a GPS! We're saved!"

The cheers! The excitement! The relief! The Derek Fitzsimmons buzzkill!

"I knew it," Derek growled, his eyes narrowing. "This is another one of your tricks, sneaky Sweet River! If we use that to get back to camp, I'll get kicked out of Outdoor Scouts for breaking the 'no technology' rule!"

Molly shook her head vigorously. "I swear it's not a trick, Derek! I'll tell them it's my device and you had nothing to do with it. The main thing is, we won't be lost anymore!"

"Oh, sure!" Derek sneered. "You're gonna 'fess up to Mr. Harrod and Mrs. Apple? I'll believe it when I see it!"

Molly was about to try again, when help came from an unlikely source. "Derek Fitzsimmons! You are impossible!" said Keiko in a fury. "If

Molly says she's gonna tell them, she's gonna tell them!"

"Yeah!" agreed Felicia, her jacket daringly unzipped all the way to her chin now. "Molly's a nice person and she would never try to get you in trouble!"

"Bubble!" came a tiny cry from the tablet, followed by "Ssshhh, Minty!"

Molly winced, but Derek was so worked up, he just kept talking. "Why are you sticking up for her? She's the enemy!"

"Oh, please, I'm so tired of the 'enemy' thing," said Keiko. "Listen, I was homesick last night and Molly went out of her way to be nice to me. She may be a Sweet, but she's actually sweet!" Keiko looked confused for a second, then shook it off. "You know what I mean!"

"Uh, *no*, I don't," said Derek. "All I know is that I'm outta here!" And he spun around on his expensive shoes and took off, disappearing into the trees.

"Derek!" cried Felicia.

Molly was shocked. "He shouldn't go off by himself!"

"Oh, let him go," scoffed Timmy and Tommy. "Let's finish the Scavenger Hunt and use Molly's GPS to get back to camp."

Rio rubbed his spiky hair anxiously. "No way we're finishing the Hunt, dudes—we need to get back and tell Mr. Harrod and Mrs. Apple about Derek!"

"Derek left his backpack!" said Felicia in horror, pointing to the bag slumped on the ground like a tired puppy. "He doesn't have any water!"

Timmy and Tommy grabbed it, looking gleeful. "Or any popcorn!" They pulled out the bag and started munching.

Rio snatched the bag away. "Not cool, guys!"

"Hey!" Timmy and Tommy snatched it back and managed to spill it all over the ground, inviting the fat squirrel and its skinnier pals to descend upon the team. "Now look what you did!"

Everyone started yelling at this point, and over the noise, Vanellope shouted, "Fighting figs on a fiddlestick, Molly! You gotta do something about this!"

Molly stuck the tablet—and her head—back inside the backpack and hissed, "I know, Vanellope! But what? Help me figure out what to do!"

Minty grabbed Vanellope by the hands. "I know exactly what they need! What *we* used to get Molly's attention!"

Vanellope's eyes lit up. "Minty! Hard to believe it, but sometimes you *do* have a helpful suggestion!"

"Right?!" Minty squealed in delight. "I'm shocked, too!"

"What?! What's the suggestion?! What do we need?!" whisper-shouted Molly.

Vanellope whirled around and flung her arms wide, looking up at Molly in excitement. And at the top of her teeny-tiny lungs, she shouted, "REEM FLERK!"

But before Molly could even get out a decent "*Huh?*" Vanellope, the other Racers, and all the icons on the home screen disappeared. Then the screen went dark.

And so did Molly's hopes.

Chapter 12

The Racers shrieked as everything around them went black, but almost immediately they found themselves surrounded by a fluffy, pearly white substance.

"Oh, dang," said Snowanna. "We got kicked to the Cloud, kids."

Vanellope whirled back to Minty, her eyes blazing. "Squinty! Miss fizz door salt!"

The Racers all looked at Vanellope in shock.

"Raging rivers of rotten rhyming, look what you've done to me!" Vanellope shouted in frustration. "What I meant was *Minty! This is your fault!*"

But Squinty—sorry, Minty—didn't seem upset. She was too busy revving up for her first big, beautiful bounce on her booty on the soft, fluffy Cloud. And after a few initial *boing*s, she hit her bouncing stride and happily started singing her own version of Snowanna's favorite disco number, "Do the Bump!"

Snowanna sighed. "I don't think that song works with the word *frump* in it, Minty."

Rancis was outraged. "Why is she so happy? Doesn't she know what just happened?" He moved closer to Minty and tried to talk to her on the way down—or up—in her bouncing. "Minty! Molly has no GPS now, and the only help we gave her was 'reem flerk'!"

The little green Racer did a flip in midair and merrily yelped, "Wheel bigger zit pout!"

"*What?!*" said Vanellope, Rancis, and Snowanna.

Surprisingly, it was Taffyta who translated this time. "*Duh*, guys. Minty said, 'She'll figure it out.' She knows Molly can handle it, and she's right. So stop stressing and let's enjoy our time in this puffy kingdom of marshmallow-ness!"

"Well. I'll be dipped in donkey sponge cake,"

said Vanellope, her anger melting away. "Taff's been right twice in one day. When has that ever happened before?"

Taffyta made a face. "Um, like, *every* day?"

"So...time to bounce and bump, y'all?" Snowanna grinned.

And the bouncing and bumping began. Vanellope performed midair splits, Rancis did a loop-de-loop with his peanut butter cup hat, Minty and Snowanna did a Bump/Frump combo, and Taffyta...

...finally got her nap.

"Reem flerk??"

Molly stared at the black screen for a moment before she realized two things: One, her battery was dead, and two, she probably should have stopped Minty's rhyming a *lonnnnggg* time ago. Oh, and now she had to explain that she actually *didn't* have an electronic device—or at least, a working one—after all. Okay, three things.

"Uh . . . Molly?" The voice was a little muffled through the canvas, but it was unmistakably Keiko's. "Why are you *in* your backpack?"

Molly cringed and slowly drew her head out. "Oh . . . uh . . . sometimes it's easier for me to think in . . . uh . . . a small, dark place."

To her relief, Keiko nodded. "Makes sense. Who could think with *that* going on?" She motioned behind her to where Timmy and Tommy were shouting "Three-second rule!" and trying to eat the popcorn off the ground before the squirrels did, and Rio was holding Felicia back from chasing after Derek into the woods as she wailed, "What if he gets stuck in quicksand?!"

Molly grimaced. "We're a hot mess."

"Yeah. I don't know what Mr. Harrod and Mrs. Apple were trying to do," Keiko said sadly. "How did they ever expect us to make this team work?"

Molly whirled around so violently Keiko took a step back. "Keiko! What did you just say?!"

"Uhhh . . ." Keiko bit her thumbnail nervously. "When?"

Molly started pacing, trying to work it out. "Team . . . work?! Team . . . 'reem'! And 'flerk' rhymes with 'work'! *That's* what she was trying to say! Because that makes the dream work! Keiko, you're a genius!"

"I am?" said Keiko, totally lost.

Molly rushed over to the group, ignoring Timmy and Tommy's "HEY!" as she stepped on some of the popcorn they were planning on eating. "Guys! I know what to do!"

Felicia stopped midwail. "You know how to save Derek from getting attacked by Bigfoot?"

"Yes!" Molly cried, then: "Wait, what? No, because there's no such thing as Big— Oh, never mind! Guys, we can find Derek, find our way back to camp, and maybe even win the Scavenger Hunt if . . . we work together as a team!"

The twins stared back at her blankly. "*That's* your big idea?" said Timmy and Tommy. "That's what you smashed our popcorn for?"

Rio shot them a look. "Dudes, not cool." Then he turned to Molly. "I get it! It's like what your father said in the camping store, right?"

"Exactly!" said Molly. "We use each of our strengths to solve this together!"

"NO. WAY," the twins said, and Molly knew they were extremely serious because Timmy said "NO" and Tommy said "WAY."

Keiko stamped her foot angrily, causing Timmy's and Tommy's eyes to go wide and the squirrels to run away clutching their popcorn crumbs in fear. "Listen up, twins of terror! We are going to do what Molly says because she's smart and because I don't plan on living out here for the rest of my life, get it?!"

They got it.

Within seconds the team had gathered and Molly wrote down their strengths on the back of the Scavenger Hunt list:

KEIKO: *Strong, knows poisonous plants, can climb trees.*

RIO: *Good friend, Halloween expert, clever thinker.*

FELICIA: *Loyal, recognizes plants that cause allergies, insect spotter.*

TIMMY & TOMMY: *Do everything together.*

MOLLY:

"Seriously?" said Timmy and Tommy, interrupting before Molly's strengths could be listed. "That's it? That's the only strength you think we have?"

Rio, Molly, Keiko, and Felicia looked at each other.

"Uh . . ." said Felicia.

"You're both . . . You have . . . You do . . ." Keiko started a sentence three times and trailed off three times.

Rio looked like his spiky hair was on fire, he was rubbing it and thinking so hard.

"You're . . . loud?" offered Molly, not sure how this was going to be received.

Timmy and Tommy looked at each other. And grinned. "YEAH! We own that!"

Molly breathed a silent sigh of relief and launched right in before the twins could reconsider. "Okay! Then Rio the 'clever thinker' will come up with the perfect jobs for all of you!"

The brain under that spiky hair worked quickly.

Timmy and Tommy were assigned to go into the woods, Tommy walking forward so he could look for Derek, Timmy walking backward and keeping track of their steps so they would know exactly how to get back. Oh, and both of them yelling "DEREK!" together (loudly, of course). Felicia was assigned to find a fuzzy dandelion (with a sneeze) and a bug (with a scream), and Keiko went along so Felicia didn't march into poison ivy.

"*Or* poison oak *or* poison sumac," said Keiko, pointing to pictures in her book. "Good to have a killer plant expert on the team, right?"

The second part of the plan started after Timmy and Tommy Lang hauled Derek out of the woods, kicking and screaming about illegal electronic devices and tomatoes disguised as sports equipment. After they patiently explained "teamwork" to Derek (and Rio promised to tell the troop leaders that Derek was a hundred percent innocent), he went to work hoisting Keiko up to the first branch of a tall tree. As Keiko climbed, she found the muddy stick (well, she stepped on a branch with her muddy boots and it broke off and landed on Derek's clean T-shirt, which didn't

go over well), something rough (an abandoned bird's nest), and a pine cone, and at the top, she peered out and shouted, "I see our campsite! I know how to get back!"

As Felicia, Rio, Timmy and Tommy, and, yes, even muddy, grumpy Derek celebrated, it suddenly occurred to Molly that they'd never written down *her* strength.

And to be honest, she *still* wasn't sure she even knew what it was.

Chapter

13

But things were very different half an hour later. Molly was standing bravely in front of both troops and Mr. Harrod and Mrs. Apple (and Mortimer, but he was asleep and snoring like a buzzsaw, so he didn't really count), and she had a message to share.

"My dad loves repeating little sayings," Molly started. "So I wasn't surprised when he told me a new one while we were shopping for camp supplies. 'Teamwork makes the dream work.'"

"What does *that* mean?" came a voice from the crowd.

Molly nodded, laughing. "That's exactly what I said! And he tried to explain it to me, that when you want to accomplish a goal with a group, you find out every person's strength and let them use it. Then you put all those strengths together and what happens is *amazeballs!*"

"Yeah, and if it hadn't been for Molly's idea to use teamwork, we'd still be lost in the woods!" called out Keiko.

Felicia made a face. "Or at least Derek would be."

"I'm innocent!" cried Derek, pounding his mud-stained chest.

"We know, we know," mumbled all the campers, since Derek had been shouting his innocence and pounding his chest for the last thirty minutes.

"I think it's time to give that a rest, Mr. Fitzsimmons," said Mr. Harrod, staring at him hard (well, as hard as a nice guy like Mr. Harrod could manage). "Molly, please continue."

Molly hesitated for a second, then decided to go for it. "*We're* all kind of a team, aren't we? We're all Outdoor Scouts, and our team's goal is to have an awesome camping trip. And I don't know what all of your strengths are, but . . ." She

grinned a little bit. "I do know what our team's *weakness* is."

And with just a wee bit more urging, the campers started coming forward, one by one, to surrender their prank materials. There were rubber spiders and lizards and snakes, a bag of birdseed to make birds attack the enemy's backpack, a Bigfoot costume (Felicia got freaked out, even though it was obviously empty), Vaseline to rub on the bathroom doorknobs, paper clips to stick through tent zippers and lock campers inside, food coloring for the showerheads, glow sticks to be cracked and poured into the toilets, face paints to decorate the enemy's face while sleeping, and shaving cream that was to be sprayed into underwear.

When it was all collected and lying in an enormous heap, which Mr. Harrod stared at in shock and Mortimer sniffed through looking for snacks, Mrs. Apple stood up and addressed the campers.

"This is truly demented," she said cheerfully,

pointing to the pile of pranks. "But a little *healthy* competition never hurt anybody. Thus, the winning Scavenger Hunt team is . . ."

A moment later, Molly, Rio, Felicia, Keiko, and Timmy and Tommy were hugging and cheering—and all the other campers cheered for them, too! Except Derek Fitzsimmons, who sat to the side with a sad look on his face as he rubbed the dried mud off his expensive T-shirt. But not for long, because Rio, Felicia, Keiko, and, yes, even Timmy and Tommy had shared something with Molly as they'd walked back to the campsite. They said that Molly's strength was caring for others and using her words to help. So, of course, she used that strength for the good of the team. The *whole* team.

"Hey, guys!" Molly called out, shushing the campers. "Mrs. Apple said we won because we were the only team that spotted one important item on the Scavenger Hunt list: animal poop."

There was laughter and groans and shouts of "Gross!" and "We didn't even *want* to see any!" from the crowd.

Molly grinned. "Well, the only reason *we* were able to find some was thanks to an overeating squirrel and the Scout who was smart enough to bring the popcorn to feed him—Derek Fitzsimmons!"

Molly started clapping toward the shocked Derek, and everyone joined in; even Timmy and Tommy broke down and shook Derek's hand (separately!) and Mortimer toddled over to lick Derek's ankle. The appreciation finally broke him, and Derek's face cracked into a smile—not the usual snooty, snarly, teeth-baring kind, but a *real* smile.

And Molly smiled, too. The only thing better than knowing your strength is knowing exactly when to use it—for the team.

C ome on, come on," mumbled Molly. She was back in her bedroom in Sweet River, sitting cross-legged on the floor next to the electrical outlet. Her tablet was plugged in and a little blinking light informed her that it was about to come back to life.

"MOLLY!" Five colorful Racers popped onto the home screen, waving wildly.

"Hi, guys!" Molly cried happily. "It's so good to see you!"

Vanellope flung her tiny arms out in delight. "Charged batteries and chocolate butterfingers, it's good to be seen!"

"So ..." said Rancis brightly. "Did we miss anything?"

Molly couldn't help but laugh. "Uh ... *yeah*." And she proceeded to tell them about figuring out "reem flerk," getting Derek back, finding all the Scavenger Hunt items, the pile of prank materials that made Mr. Harrod's eyes bug out, her speech, being the winners, her new friendship with Keiko and Felicia, and figuring out her own strengths, of course.

"Well, *doyyyy*, Molly," said Vanellope. "*We* knew that your strength was caring for others and using helpful words. We're glad that Kanye and Ferdinand saw it, too, so y'all can be friends."

Molly gulped. "Well . . . now I have to use my words to say something kinda hard . . ."

Very slowly, she told the Racers that when she'd gotten home from the camping trip, her mom was happy about something—the renovation at Litwak's Family Fun Center was done ahead of schedule. "So . . . if you like . . . I can take you back there tonight and plug you back in to Game Central Station. . . . But, you know, if you want to stay a little bit longer . . . that'd be good, too."

The Racers took this information in quietly. Vanellope rubbed her head, sending tiny candies flying all over the home screen. Rancis tugged at the sleeves of his chocolate-brown suit anxiously. Snowanna took the Popsicle stick out of her hair and examined it like the snow-cone colors could predict the future. Minty adjusted her mint green leg warmers even though they were already perfectly even. Taffyta sucked so hard on her lolly, her cheeks went concave.

Molly smiled, only a little bit sadly. "You want to go home."

Rancis peeked up at her from under the brim of his peanut butter cup hat. "I love hanging out with you, Molly. It's just . . . I miss doing guy stuff with Gloyd and Swizzle."

"And I miss driving superfast and running Minty's car off the road into Caramel Canyon," whispered Snowanna. She turned to Minty, "You, too?"

Minty nodded. "Be, loo."

"Mom has an all-black uniform," said Taffyta, a single mascara-d tear dripping out at the memory of Sergeant Calhoun. "So when I cry on her, you can't even see it."

Vanellope peered up at Molly. "You're our bestie, Moll. But I sure would like to hang out with Ralph for a hot minute before I go back to Shank, Pyro, and Butcher Boy."

"I understand, guys, I really do," said Molly. "I just . . . wish you could be in both places."

The Racers nodded. Suddenly:

"We *can* be in both places!" exclaimed Minty. "We can go home today, but anytime Molly wants to take us on an adventure, she can come to Litwak's and plug her tablet into Game Central Station! It's the best of both worlds!"

The other Racers and Molly stared at Minty, stunned.

Vanellope finally found her voice. "Well, I'll be double dunked in a Dairy Queen blizzard," she said in awe. "Minty, maybe your strength really *is* giving helpful suggestions instead of rhyming!"

Minty jumped up and down in excitement. "Bless! Chess!"

The Racers and Molly sighed. "Well, it was nice while it lasted," said Vanellope.

So, it was decided. Molly would return them to *Sugar Rush*, but anytime she got lonely or needed her five BFFs, the Racers would be ready to *swooooosh* through the power cord onto Molly's home screen and go on another wild adventure. Molly held her finger up for five tiny high-ones (fingertip to palm).

"Sweet Molly of monkey milk," Vanellope said, beaming. "You're the best."

"Totally!" said Snowanna. "Thanks for taking care of five crazy-cool kids from an alternate universe!"

Rancis tipped his peanut butter cup hat. "Molly, your *heart* is a superstrong muscle."

Minty clapped her hands together. "Pee glove poo!"

"Um, yeah, what they all said," mumbled Taffyta.

The Racers gave her a look.

"What? You know I'm not good with raw emotion!" Taffyta whined.

"Baffyta . . ." Minty rhymed in a threatening voice.

Taffyta pursed her extra-pink lips. "Fine, fine, fine. What Minty said before. You know . . . 'pee glove poo.'"

Molly winked at Taffyta and smiled softly at her five besties. "I love you, too."